DEAD MEN WORKING IN THE CANE FIELDS

BY

W. B. SEABROOK

British Library Cataloguing-in-Publication Data
A catalogue record for this book is available from the
British Library

CONTENTS

W. B. SEABROOK

William Buehler Seabrook was born in Westminster, Maryland in 1886. He received his education at Mercersburg Academy in Pennsylvania, Roanoke College in Virginia and Newberry College in South Carolina. A few days after graduating, Seabrook walked into the newspaper offices of the *Augusta Chronicle* in Georgia, and talked his way into a job. Within months he went from a reporter to city editor, but in 1908 he abruptly moved to Switzerland, where he studied philosophy and metaphysics at the University of Geneva. After graduating, Seabrook drifted around Europe for nearly two years, and in 1915 he joined the French Army. During World War I, he was gassed at Verdun, and was later awarded the Croix de Guerre.

After the war, in New York, Seabrook made his start as a writer. Under the encouragement of H. L. Mencken, he began to write news and features for a number of syndicates, including *The New York Times, Cosmopolitan, Reader's Digest* and *Vanity Fair*. His career of travel and adventure – for which he would eventually be famed – began in 1924, with a trip to Arabia which later became his first book, *Adventures in Arabia* (1927). Seabrook followed this up with *The Magic Island* (1929), a book about voodoo worshippers in Haiti, and then his infamous *Jungle Ways* (1930), in which he detailed his time spent with West African cannibals, and his experience of sampling human flesh.

In December 1933, Seabrook was committed at his own request to Bloomingdale, a mental institution near New York City, for treatment for acute alcoholism. He remained here for a year, and recounted his experiences in the 1935 non-fiction work, *Asylum*, which became a bestseller. During the late thirties and early forties he published four more novels, before committing suicide by drug overdose in Rhinebeck, New York, shortly before the end of World War II.

DEAD MEN WORKING IN THE CANE FIELDS

W. B. Seabrook

Pretty mulatto Julie had taken baby Marianne to bed. Constant Polynice and I sat late before the doorway of his *caille*, talking of fire-hags, demons, werewolves, and vampires, while a full moon, rising slowly, flooded his sloping cotton-fields and the dark rolling hills beyond.

Polynice was a Haitian farmer, but he was no common jungle peasant. He lived on the island of La Gonave, where I shall return to him in later stories. He seldom went over to the Haitian mainland, but he knew what was going on in Port-au-Prince, and spoke sometimes of installing a radio. A countryman, half peasant born and bred, he was familiar with every superstition of the mountains and the plain, yet too intelligent to believe them literally true – or at least so I gathered from his talk.

He was interested in helping me toward an understanding of the tangled Haitian folk-lore. It was only by chance that we came presently to a subject which – though I refused for a long time to admit it – lies in a baffling category on the ragged edge of things which are beyond either superstition or reason. He had been telling me of fire-hags who left their skins at home and set the canefields blazing; of the vampire, a woman sometimes living, sometimes dead, who sucked the blood of children and who could be distinguished because her hair always turned an ugly red; of the werewolf – *chauché*, in creole – a man or woman who took the form of some animal, usually a dog, and went killing lambs, young goats, sometimes babies.

All this, I gathered, he considered to be pure superstition, as he told me with tolerant scorn how his friend and neighbour Osmann had one night seen a grey dog slinking with bloody jaws from his sheep-pen, and who, after having shot and exorcised and buried it, was so convinced he had killed a certain girl named Liane who was generally reputed to be a *chauché* that when he met her two days later on the path to Grande Source he believed she was a ghost come back for vengeance, and fled howling.

As Polynice talked on, I reflected that these tales ran closely parallel not only with those of the negroes in Georgia and the Carolinas, but with the medieval folk-lore of white Europe. Werewolves, vampires, and demons were certainly no novelty. But I recalled one creature I had been hearing about in Haiti, which sounded exclusively local – the zombie.

It seemed (or so I had been assured by negroes more credulous than Polynice) that while the zombie came from the grave, it was neither a ghost nor yet a person who had been raised like Lazarus from the dead. The zombie, they say, is a soulless human corpse, still dead, but taken from the grave and endowed by sorcery with a mechanical semblance of life – it is a dead body which is made to walk and act and move as if it were alive. People who have the power to do this go to a fresh grave, dig up the body before it has had time to rot, galvanize it into movement, and then make of it a servant or slave, occasionally for the commission of some crime, more often simply as a drudge around the habitation or the farm, setting it dull heavy tasks, and beating it like a dumb beast if it slackens.

As this was revolving in my mind, I said to Polynice: 'It seems to me that these werewolves and vampires are first cousins to those we have at home, but I have never, except in Haiti, heard of anything like zombies. Let us talk of them for a little while. I wonder if you can tell me something of this zombie superstition. I should like to get at some idea of how it originated.'

My rational friend Polynice was deeply astonished. He leaned over and put his hand in protest on my knee.

'Superstition? But I assure you that this of which you now speak is not a matter of superstition. Alas, these things – and other evil practices connected with the dead – exist. They exist to an extent that you whites do not dream of, though there is evidence everywhere under your eyes.

'Why do you suppose that even the poorest peasants, when they can, bury their dead beneath solid tombs of masonry? Why do they bury them so often in their own yards, close to the doorway? Why, so often, do you see a tomb or grave set close beside a busy road or footpath where people are always passing? It is to assure the poor unhappy dead such protection as we can.

'I will take you in the morning to see the grave of my brother, who was killed in the way you know. It is over there on the little ridge which you can see clearly now in the moonlight, open space all round it, close beside the trail which everybody passes going to and from Grande Source. For four nights we watched there, in the peristyle, Osmann and I, with shotguns – for at that time both my dead brother and I had bitter enemies – until we were sure the body had begun to rot.

'No, my friend, no, no. There are only too many true cases. At this very moment, in the moonlight, there are zombies working on this island, less than two hours' ride from my own habitation. We know about them, but we do not dare to interfere so long as our own dead are left unmolested. If you will ride with me tomorrow night, yes, I will show you dead men working in the canefields. Close even to the cities there are sometimes zombies. Perhaps you have already heard of those that were at Hasco . . .'

'What about Hasco?' I interrupted him, for in the whole of Haiti, Hasco is perhaps the last name anybody would think of connecting with either sorcery or superstition. The word is American-commercial-synthetic, like Nabisco, Delco, Socony. It stands for the Haitian-American Sugar Company – an immense factory plant, dominated by a huge chimney, with clanging machinery, steam whistles, freight cars. It is like a chunk of Hoboken. It lies in the eastern suburbs of Port-au-Prince, and beyond it stretch the canefields of the Cul-de-Sac. Hasco makes rum when the sugar market is off, pays low wages, a shilling or so a day, and gives steady work. It is modern big business, and it sounds it, looks it, smells it.

Such, then, was the incongruous background for the weird tale Constant Polynice now told me.

The spring of 1918 was a big cane season, and the factory, which had its own plantations, offered a bonus on the wages of new workers. Soon heads of families and villages from the mountain and the plain came trailing their ragtag little armies, men, women, children, trooping to the registration bureau and thence into the fields.

One morning an old black headman, Ti Joseph of Colombier, appeared leading a band of ragged creatures who shuffled along behind him, staring dumbly, like people walking in a daze. As Joseph lined them up for registration, they still stared, vacant-eyed like cattle, and made no reply when asked to give their names.

Joseph said they were ignorant people from the slopes of Morne-au-Diable, a roadless mountain district near the Dominican border, and that they did not understand the creole of the plains. They were frightened, he said, by the din and smoke of the great factory, but under his direction they would work hard in the fields. The farther they were sent away from the factory, from the noise and bustle of the railway yards, the better it would be.

Better, indeed, for these were not living men and women but poor unhappy zombies whom Joseph and his wife Croyance had dragged from their peaceful graves to slave for him in the sun – and if by chance a brother or father of the dead should see and recognise them, Joseph knew that it would mean trouble for him.

So they were assigned to distant fields beyond the crossroads, and camped there, keeping to themselves like any proper family or village group; but in the evening when other little companies, encamped apart as they were, gathered each around its one big common pot of savoury millet or plantains, generously seasoned with dried fish and garlic, Croyance would tend *two* pots upon the fire, for, as everyone knows, the zombies must never be permitted to taste salt or meat. So the food prepared for them was tasteless and unseasoned.

As the zombies toiled day after day dumbly in the sun, Joseph sometimes beat them to make them move faster, but Croyance began to pity the poor dead creatures who should be at rest – and pitied them in the evenings when she dished out their flat, tasteless *bouillie*.

Each Saturday afternoon Joseph went to collect the wages for them all, and what division he made was no concern of Hasco, so long as the work went forward. Sometimes Joseph alone, and sometimes Croyance alone, went to Croix de Bouquet for the Saturday night *bamboche* or the Sunday cockfight, but always one of them remained with the zombies to prepare their food and see that they did not stray away.

Through February this continued, until Fête Dieu approached, with a Saturday-Sunday-Monday holiday for all the workers. Joseph, with his pockets full of money, went to Port-au-Prince and left Croyance behind, cautioning her as usual; and she agreed to remain and tend the zombies, for he promised her that at the Mardi Gras she should visit the city.

But when Sunday morning dawned it was lonely in the fields, and her kind old woman's heart was filled with pity for the zombies, and she thought, 'Perhaps it will cheer them a little to see the gay crowds and the processions at Croix de Bouquet, and since all the Morne-au-Diable people will have gone back to the mountain to celebrate Fête Dieu at home, no one will recognize them, and no harm can come of it.' And it is true that Croyance also wished to see the gay procession.

So she tied a new bright-coloured handkerchief round her head, aroused the zombies from the sleep that was scarcely different from their waking, gave them their morning bowl of cold, unsalted plantains boiled in water, which they ate dumbly uncomplaining, and set out with them for the town, single file, as the country people always walk. Croyance, in her bright kerchief, leading the nine dead men and women behind her, passed the railroad crossing, where she murmured a prayer to Legba, passed the great white-painted wooden Christ, who hung life-sized in the glaring sun, where she stopped to kneel and cross herself – but the poor zombies prayed neither to Papa Legba nor to Brother Jesus, for they were dead bodies walking, without souls or minds.

They followed her to the market square before the church, where hundreds of little thatched, open shelters, used on weekdays for buying and selling, were empty of trade, but crowded here and there by gossiping groups in the grateful shade.

To the shade of one of these market booths, which was still unoccupied, she led the zombies, and they sat like people asleep with their eyes open, staring, but seeing nothing, as the bells in the church began to ring, and the procession came from the priest's house – red-purple robes, golden crucifix held aloft, tinkling bells and swinging incense-pots, followed by little black boys in white lace robes, little black girls in starched white dresses, with shoes and stockings, from the parish school, with coloured ribbons in their kinky hair, a nun beneath a big umbrella leading them.

Croyance knelt with the throng as the procession passed, and wished she might follow it across the square to the church steps, but the zombies just sat and stared, seeing nothing.

When noontime came, women with baskets passed to and fro in the crowd, or sat selling little sweet cakes, figs (which were not figs but sweet bananas), oranges, dried herring, biscuit, casava bread, and *clairin* poured from a bottle at a penny a glass.

As Croyance sat with her savoury dried herring and biscuit baked with salt and soda, and provision of *clairin* in the tin cup by her side, she pitied the zombies who had worked so faithfully for Joseph in the canefields, and who now had nothing, while all the other groups around were feasting, and as she pitied them, a woman passed crying:

'*Tablettes! Tablettes pistaches! T'ois pour dix cobs!*'

Tablettes are a sort of candy made of brown cane sugar (*rapadou*); sometimes with *pistaches*, which in Haiti are peanuts, or with coriander seed. And Croyance thought, 'These *tablettes* are not salted or seasoned, they are sweet, and can do no harm to the zombies just this once.' So she untied the corner of her kerchief, took out a coin, a *gourdon*, the quarter of a *gourde*, and bought some of the *tablettes*, which she broke in halves and divided among the zombies, who began sucking and mumbling them in their mouths. But the baker of the *tablettes* had salted the *pistache* nuts before stirring them into the *rapadou*, and as the zombies tasted the salt, they knew they were dead and made a dreadful outcry and rose and turned their faces toward the mountain.

No one dared to stop them, for they were corpses walking in the sunlight, and they themselves and everyone else knew that they were corpses. And they disappeared toward the mountain.

When later they drew near their own village on the slopes of Morne-au-Diable, these men and women walking single file in the twilight, with no soul leading them or daring to follow, the people of their village, who were also holding *bamboche* in the market-place, saw them drawing closer, recognized among them fathers, brothers, wives, and daughters whom they had buried months before. Most of them knew at once the truth, that these were zombies who had been dragged dead from their graves, but others hoped that a blessed miracle had taken place on this Fête Dieu, and rushed forward to take them in their arms and welcome them.

But the zombies shuffled through the market-place, recognizing neither father nor wife nor mother, and as they turned leftward up the path leading to the graveyard, a woman whose daughter was in the procession of the dead threw herself screaming before the girl's shuffling feet and begged her to stay; but the grave-cold feet of the daughter and the feet of the other dead shuffled over her and onward; and as they approached the graveyard, they began to shuffle faster and rushed among the graves, and each before his own empty grave began clawing at the stones and earth to enter it again; and as their cold hands touched the earth of their own graves, they fell and lay there, rotting carrion.

That night the fathers, sons, and brothers of the zombies, after restoring the bodies to their graves, sent a messenger on muleback down the mountain, who returned next day with the name of Ti Joseph and with a stolen shirt of Ti Joseph's which had been worn next to his skin and was steeped in the grease-sweat of his body.

They collected silver in the village, and went with the name of Ti Joseph and the shirt of Ti Joseph to a *bocor* beyond Trou Caiman, who made a deadly needle *ouanga*, a black bag *ouanga*, pierced all through with pins and needles, filled with dry goat dung, circled with cock's feathers dipped in blood. And in case the needle *ouanga* be slow in working or be rendered weak by Joseph's counter-magic, they sent men down to the plain, who lay in wait patiently for Joseph, and one night hacked off his head with a machete . . .

When Polynice had finished this recital, I said to him, after a moment of silence, 'You are not a peasant like those of the Cul-de-Sac; you are a reasonable man, or at least it seems to me you are. Now, how much of that story, honestly, do you believe?'

He replied earnestly: 'I did not see these special things, but there were many witnesses, and why should I not believe them when I myself have also seen zombies? When you also have seen them, with their faces and their eyes in which there is no life, you will not only believe in these zombies who should be resting in their graves, you will pity them from the bottom of your heart.'

Before finally taking leave of La Gonave, I did see these 'walking dead men', and I did, in a sense, believe in them and pitied them, indeed, from the bottom of my heart. It was not the next night, though Polynice, true to his promise, rode with me across the Plaine Mapou to the deserted, silent canefields where he had hoped to show me zombies labouring. It was not on any night. It was in broad daylight one afternoon, when we passed that way again, on the lower trail to Picmy. Polynice reined in his horse and pointed to a rough, stony, terraced slope – on which four labourers, three men and a woman, were chopping the earth with machetes, among straggling cotton stalks, a hundred yards distant from the trail.

'Wait while I go up there,' he said, excited because a chance had come to fulfil his promise. 'I think it is Lamercie with the zombies. If I wave to you, leave your horse and come.' Starting up the slope, he shouted to the woman, 'It is I, Polynice,' and when he waved later, I followed.

As I clambered up, Polynice was talking to the woman. She had stopped work – a big-boned, hard-faced black girl, who regarded us with surly unfriendliness. My first impression of the three supposed zombies, who continued dumbly to work, was that there was something about them which was unnatural and strange. They were plodding like brutes, like automatons. Without stooping down, I could not fully see their faces, which were bent expressionless over their work. Polynice touched one of them on the shoulder and motioned him to get up. Obediently, like an animal, he slowly stood erect – and what I saw then, coupled with what I had heard previously, or despite it, came as a rather sickening shock. The eyes were the worst. It was not my imagination. They were in truth like the eyes of a dead man, not blind, but staring, unfocused, unseeing. The whole face, for that matter, was bad enough. It was vacant, as if there was nothing behind it. It seemed not only expressionless, but incapable of expression. I had seen so much previously in Haiti that was outside ordinary normal experience that for the flash of a second I had a sickening, almost panicky lapse in which I thought, or rather felt, 'Great God, maybe this stuff is really true, and if it is true, it is rather awful, for it upsets everything.' By 'everything' I meant the natural fixed laws and processes on which all modern human thought and actions are based. Then suddenly I remembered – and my mind seized the memory as a man sinking in water clutches a solid plank – the face of a dog I had once seen in the histological laboratory at Columbia. Its entire front brain had been removed in an experimental operation weeks before; it moved about, it was alive, but its eyes were like the eyes I now saw staring.

I recovered from my mental panic. I reached out and grasped one of the dangling hands. It was calloused, solid, human. Holding it, I said, *'Bonjour, compère.'* The zombie stared without responding. The black wench, Lamercie, who was their keeper, now more sullen than ever, pushed me away – *'Z'affai' nèg pas z'affai' blanc'* (Negroes' affairs are not for whites). But I had seen enough. 'Keeper' was the key to it. 'Keeper' was the word that had leapt naturally into my mind as she protested, and just as naturally the zombies were nothing but poor ordinary demented human beings, idiots, forced to toil in the fields.

It was a good rational explanation, but it is far from being the end of this story. It satisfied me then, and I said as much to Polynice as we went down the slope. At first he did not contradict me, even said doubtfully, 'Perhaps'; but as we reached the horses, before mounting, he stopped and said, 'Look here, I respect your distrust of what you call superstition and your desire to find out the truth, but if what you were saying now were the whole truth, how could it be that over and over again people who have stood by and seen their own relatives buried, have, sometimes soon, sometimes months or years afterwards, found those relatives working as zombies, and have sometimes killed the man who held them in servitude?'

'Polynice,' I said, 'that's just the part of it that I can't believe. The zombies in such cases may have resembled the dead persons, or even been "doubles" – you know what doubles are, how two people resemble each other to a startling degree. But it is a fixed rule of reasoning in my country that we will never accept the possibility of a thing being "supernatural" so long as any natural explanation, even far-fetched, seems adequate.'

'Well,' said he, 'if you spent many years in Haiti, you would find it very hard to fit this reasoning into some of the things you encountered here.'

As I have said, there is more to this story – and I think it is best to tell it very simply.

In all Haiti there is no clearer scientifically trained mind, no sounder pragmatic rationalist, than Dr Antoine Villiers. When I sat with him in his study, surrounded by hundreds of scientific books in French, German, and English, and told him of what I had seen and of my conversations with Polynice, he said:

'My dear sir, I do not believe in miracles nor in supernatural events, and I do not want to shock your Anglo-Saxon intelligence, but this Polynice of yours, with all his superstition, may have been closer to the partial truth than you were. Understand me clearly. I do not believe that anyone has ever been raised literally from the dead – neither Lazarus, nor the daughter of Jairus, nor Jesus Christ himself – yet I am not sure, paradoxical as it may sound, that there is not something frightful, something in the nature of criminal sorcery if you like, in some cases at least, in this matter of zombies. I am by no means sure that some of them who now toil in the fields were not dragged from the actual graves in which they lay in their coffins, buried by their mourning families!'

'It is then something like suspended animation?' I asked.

'I will show you,' he replied, 'a thing which may supply the key to what you are seeking,' and standing on a chair, he pulled down a paper-bound book from a top shelf. It was nothing mysterious or esoteric. It was the current official *Code Pénal* (Criminal Code) of the Republic of Haiti. He thumbed through it and pointed to a paragraph which read:

'Article 249. Also shall be qualified as attempted murder the employment which may be made against any person of substances which, without causing actual death, produce a lethargic coma more or less prolonged. If, after the administering of such substances, the person has been buried, the act shall be considered murder no matter what result follows.'

The strangest and most chimeric story of this type ever related to me in Haiti by Haitians who claimed direct knowledge of its essential truth is the tale of Matthieu Toussel's mad bride, the tale of how her madness came upon her. I shall try to reconstruct it here as it was told to me – as it was dramatized, elaborated, perhaps, in the oft re-telling.

An elderly and respected Haitian gentleman whose wife was French had a young niece, by name Camille, a fair-skinned octoroon girl whom they introduced and sponsored in Port-au-Prince society, where she became popular, and for whom they hoped to arrange a brilliant marriage.

Her own family, however, was poor; her uncle, it was understood, could scarcely be expected to dower her – he was prosperous, but not wealthy, and had a family of his own – and the French *dot* system prevails in Haiti, so that while the young beaux of the élite crowded to fill her dance-cards, it became gradually evident that none of them had serious intentions.

When she was nearing the age of twenty, Matthieu Toussel, a rich coffee-grower from Morne Hôpital, became a suitor, and presently asked her hand in marriage. He was dark and more than twice her age, but rich, suave, and well-educated. The principal house of the Toussel habitation, on the mountainside almost overlooking Port-au-Prince, was not thatched, mud-walled, but a fine wooden bungalow, slate-roofed, with wide verandahs, set in a garden among gay poinsettias, palms, and Bougainvillaea vines. He had built a road there, kept his own big motorcar, and was often seen in the fashionable cafés and clubs.

There was an old rumour that he was affiliated in some way with Voodoo or sorcery, but such rumours are current concerning almost every Haitian who has acquired power in the mountains, and in the case of men like Toussel are seldom taken seriously. He asked no *dot*, he promised to be generous, both to her and her straitened family, and the family persuaded her into the marriage.

The black planter took his pale girl-bride back with him to the mountain, and for almost a year, it appears, she was not unhappy, or at least gave no signs of it. They still came down to Port-au-Prince, appeared occasionally at the club soirées. Toussel permitted her to visit her family whenever she liked, lent her father money, and arranged to send her young brother to a school in France.

But gradually her family, and her friends as well, began to suspect that all was not going so happily up yonder as it seemed. They began to notice that she was nervous in her husband's presence, that she seemed to have acquired a vague, growing dread of him. They wondered if Toussel were ill-treating or neglecting her. The mother sought to gain her daughter's confidence, and the girl gradually opened her heart. No, her husband had never ill-treated her, never a harsh word; he was always kindly and considerate, but there were nights when he seemed strangely preoccupied, and on such nights he would saddle his horse and ride away into the hills, sometimes not returning until after dawn, when he seemed even stranger and more lost in his own thoughts than on the night before. And there was something in the way he sometimes sat staring at her which made her feel that she was in some way connected with those secret thoughts.

She was afraid of his thoughts and afraid of him. She knew intuitively, as women know, that no other woman was involved in these nocturnal excursions. She was not jealous. She was in the grip of an unreasoning fear. One morning, when she thought he had been away all night in the hills, chancing to look out of a window, so she told her mother, she had seen him emerging from the door of a low frame building in their own big garden, set at some distance from the others and which he had told her was his office where he kept his accounts, his business papers, and the door always locked . . . 'So, therefore,' said the mother relieved and reassured, 'what does all this amount to? Business troubles, those secret thoughts of his, probably . . . some coffee combination he is planning and which is perhaps going wrong, so that he sits up all night at his desk figuring and devising, or rides off to sit up half the night consulting with others. Men are like that. It explains itself. The rest of it is nothing but your nervous imagining.'

And this was the last rational talk the mother and daughter ever had. What subsequently occurred up there on the fatal night of their first wedding anniversary they pieced together from the half-lucid intervals of a terrorised, cowering, hysterical creature, who finally went stark, raving mad. But what she had gone through was indelibly stamped on her brain; there were early periods when she seemed quite sane, and the sequential tragedy was gradually evolved.

On the evening of their anniversary Toussel had ridden away, telling her not to sit up for him, and she had assumed that in his preoccupation he had forgotten the date, which hurt her and made her silent. She went away to bed early, and finally fell asleep.

Near midnight she was awakened by her husband, who stood at the bedside, holding a lamp. He must have been some time returned, for he was fully dressed now in formal evening clothes.

'Put on your wedding dress and make yourself beautiful,' he said; 'we are going to a party.' She was sleepy and dazed, but innocently pleased, imagining that a belated recollection of the date had caused him to plan a surprise for her. She supposed he was taking her to a late supper-dance down at the club by the seaside, where people often appeared long after midnight. 'Take your time,' he said, 'and make yourself as beautiful as you can – there is no hurry.'

An hour later when she joined him on the verandah, she said, 'But where is the car?'

'No,' he replied, 'the party is to take place here.' She noticed that there were lights in the outbuilding, the 'office' across the garden. He gave her no time to question or protest. He seized her arm, led her through the dark garden, and opened the door. The office, if it had ever been one, was transformed into a dining room, softly lighted with tall candles. There was a big old-fashioned buffet with a mirror and cut-glass bowls, plates of cold meats and salads, bottles of wine and decanters of rum.

In the centre of the room was an elegantly set table with damask cloth, flowers, glittering silver. Four men, also in evening clothes, but badly fitting, were already seated at this table. There were two vacant chairs at its head and foot. The seated men did not rise when the girl in her bride-clothes entered on her husband's arm. They sat slumped down in their chairs and did not even turn their heads to greet her. There were wine-glasses partly filled before them, and she thought they were already drunk.

As she sat down mechanically in the chair to which Toussel led her, seating himself facing her, with the four guests ranged between them, two on either side, he said, in an unnatural, strained way, the stress increasing as he spoke:

'I beg you . . . to forgive my guests their . . . seeming rudeness. It has been a long time . . . since . . . they have . . . tasted wine . . . sat like this at table . . . with . . . so fair a hostess . . . But, ah, presently . . . they will drink with you, yes . . . lift . . . their arms, as I lift mine . . . clink glasses with you . . . more . . . they will arise and . . . . dance with you . . . more . . . they will . . .'

Near her, the black fingers of one silent guest were clutched rigidly around the fragile stem of a wine-glass, tilted, spilling. The horror pent up in her overflowed. She seized a candle, thrust it close to the slumped, bowed face, and saw the man was dead. She was sitting at a banquet table with four propped-up corpses!

Breathless for an instant, then screaming, she leaped to her feet and ran. Toussel reached the door too late to seize her. He was heavy and more than twice her age. She ran still screaming across the dark garden, flashing white among the trees, out through the gate. Youth and utter terror lent wings to her feet, and she escaped . . .

A procession of early market-women, with their laden baskets and donkeys, winding down the mountainside at dawn, found her lying unconscious far below, at the point where the jungle trail emerged into the road. Her flimsy dress was ripped and torn, her little white satin bride-slippers were scuffed and stained, one of the high heels ripped off where she had caught it in a vine and fallen.

They bathed her face to revive her, bundled her on a pack-donkey, walking beside her, holding her. She was only half-conscious, incoherent, and they began disputing among themselves as peasants do. Some thought she was a French lady who had been thrown or fallen from a motor car; others thought she was a *Dominicaine*, which has been synonymous in creole from earliest colonial days with 'fancy prostitute'. None recognised her as Madame Toussel; perhaps none of them had ever seen her. They were discussing and disputing whether to leave her at a hospital of Catholic sisters on the outskirts of the city, which they were approaching, or whether it would be safer – for them – to take her directly to police headquarters and tell their story. Their loud disputing seemed to rouse her; she seemed partially to recover her senses and understand what they were saying. She told them her name, her maiden family name, and begged them to take her to her father's house.

There, put to bed and with doctors summoned, the family were able to gather from the girl's hysterical utterances a partial comprehension of what had happened. They sent up that same day to confront Toussel if they could – to search his habitation. But Toussel was gone, and all the servants were gone except one old man, who said that Toussel was in Santo Domingo. They broke into the so-called office, and found there the table still set for six people, wine spilled on the table-cloth, a bottle overturned, chairs knocked over, the platters of food still untouched on the sideboard, but beyond that they found nothing.

Toussel never returned to Haiti. It is said that he is living now in Cuba. Criminal pursuit was useless. What reasonable hope could they have had of convicting him on the unsupported evidence of a wife of unsound mind?

And there, as it was related to me, the story trailed off to a shrugging of the shoulders, to mysterious inconclusion.

What had this Toussel been planning – what sinister, perhaps criminal necromancy in which his bride was to be the victim or the instrument? What would have happened if she had not escaped?

I asked these questions, but got no convincing explanation or even theory in reply. There are tales of rather ghastly abominations, unprintable, practised by certain sorcerers who claim to raise the dead, but so far as I know they are only tales. And as for what actually did happen that night, credibility depends on the evidence of a demented girl.

So what is left?

What is left may be stated in a single sentence:

Matthieu Toussel arranged a wedding anniversary supper for his bride at which six plates were laid, and when she looked into the faces of his four other guests, she went mad.

www.ingramcontent.com/pod-product-compliance
Lightning Source LLC
Chambersburg PA
CBHW030544180626
46810CB00005B/1994